MUPPET KIDS™ IN
Piggy Gets the Jitters

By Louise Gikow

Illustrated by Tom Cooke

Muppet Press

"And one and two and three and four...."

Piggy's piano teacher, Ms. Hickory, counted out the beats as Piggy played her exercises.

"That was very good," said Ms. Hickory when Piggy had finished. "Now, don't forget, dear. The piano recital is next Sunday at three o'clock. Have you picked out a piece that you'd like to play?"

Picked out a piece! Piggy groaned to herself as she walked home. *What am I going to do?*

Piggy wouldn't admit it to anyone, but she was terrified of playing the piano in front of an audience.

I'll make billions of mistakes, she worried. I'm not any good at all...not like Rowlf. All the practicing in the world won't help. I'll make a fool out of myself next Sunday...I just know it.

The next day in school, Rowlf came up to her during lunch. "Hi, Piggy," he said. "Do you know what you're doing for the recital next Sunday?"

"Oh...uh...gee!" said Piggy. "I...think I have something I have to do on Sunday. Like...uh...iron my socks. I don't think my mom's going to let me go to the recital at all."

"Gee, that's too bad," said Rowlf. "I have a great piece picked out. It's going to be fun!"

How can Rowlf think that playing in front of all those people can be fun? Piggy wondered as she walked home from school with Skeeter and Janice later that day. *All it is is scary.*

"Hey, Piggy," said Skeeter, interrupting Piggy's gloomy thoughts. "You've been awfully quiet. Is there anything wrong?"

Piggy started. "No," she said quickly. "Nothing. Nothing at all." She wasn't going to admit for a second that she was afraid.

But what was she going to do?

For the next few days, all Piggy could think about was finding a way out of her recital.

She played softball every afternoon with Kermit and the gang, hoping she'd sprain her wrist.

But all that happened was that she hit five home runs and her team won every game.

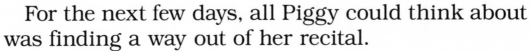

She went outside in the rain without an umbrella, hoping that she'd get a cold.

But when her mom took her temperature, it was perfectly normal.

By Friday, Piggy was very scared. And what was worse, she had spent so much time trying to figure a way out of her recital, she hadn't practiced the piano once.

After school, Piggy was sitting on a swing in the park when Rowlf wandered by.

"Hi, Piggy," he said. "You ready for the recital?"

Piggy felt something inside her go plunk. "Oh, Rowlf!" she cried. "What am I going to do?"

"About what?" Rowlf asked.

"I…uh…oh, I might as well tell you. I haven't practiced all week. I haven't slept all week. I don't want to play in the recital. I'm too scared!"

"Gee, Piggy. What are you scared about? Recitals are fun!" Rowlf said.

"Maybe for you," Piggy groaned. "You play really well. But I just know I'll make a fool out of myself in front of all those people."

Rowlf nodded. "I think I understand," he said. "You're suffering from a massive case of stage fright."

"What can I do?" Piggy asked tearfully.

"Come over to my house," Rowlf suggested. "Maybe I can help."

When Piggy and Rowlf got there, Rowlf poured them each a glass of milk. Then they sat at the kitchen table and talked.

"Look," said Rowlf. "What's the absolutely, positively worst thing that could happen?"

"I'll be terrible, and everyone will laugh at me," Piggy said in a very small voice.

"And is that really so awful?" Rowlf said.

"Of course it is," said Piggy. "Isn't it?"

Rowlf shook his head. "Think about it," he said. "Sure, you'd feel bad for a while. But nothing would really change. We'd still be your friends. Your mom would still love you."

Piggy began to feel a little better.

"There's another thing, though," Rowlf went on.
"Come on." He led Piggy over to his piano.

"You know, you don't have to make lots of
mistakes at all if you do one very important thing,"
he told her.

"What's that?" Piggy asked eagerly.

"Practice," Rowlf said.

So that's what Piggy did for the rest of the afternoon. Rowlf helped her pick out a nice, simple piece,
and they worked on it together.

Then Piggy went home. And all that evening and the next day, she stayed home and practiced. Even when Kermit came by and asked her to go for a walk, she didn't leave the piano bench. As a matter of fact, Kermit decided to stay and listen for a while.

"Sounds great, Piggy," he said. "You're going to be terrific tomorrow."

"I hope so," said Piggy, feeling a little flutter in her stomach.

The next day, Piggy woke up really early. Her insides felt sort of tickly. For a moment, she didn't know why. But then she remembered the recital.

Well, she thought, taking a deep breath, *I practiced as much as I could, and I know my piece. Now I just have to try my best.*

Piggy got all dressed up and ready to go. *I can do it,* she kept repeating to herself. *I know I can do it.*

The piano recital was being held at Ms. Hickory's music studio. Piggy's friends were all in the audience, and Rowlf had saved her a seat in the front row with the other piano students.

"How are you feeling?" he whispered to her as she sat down.

"Nervous," Piggy admitted.

"That's only natural," Rowlf said, grinning encouragingly at her. "So am I. But I know you'll be great."

"Maybe not great," Piggy said, and smiled a little. "But I'll be okay."

When Piggy got up to play, her mouth was dry.
She sat down at the piano and looked out at the
audience. All her friends smiled up at her.

For a second she closed her eyes in a panic. Then
she took a deep breath. *I can do it,* she said to
herself. *I practiced hard. I know I can do it.*

And then she put her fingers on the keys and began to play.

Piggy's performance wasn't perfect. But it was pretty good. And a funny thing happened. As she played, Piggy actually began to enjoy herself a little. She started to feel lots of good feelings coming to her from her friends in the audience. They wanted her to do well. And that made everything easier.

When Piggy had finally finished, everybody clapped and clapped. She stood up and took a bow.

"I'm very proud of you, Piggy," said Ms. Hickory. "You gave a lovely performance." That made Piggy feel good. But what made her feel even better was being proud of herself.

Gee, thought Piggy. *That wasn't so bad. In fact, I sort of liked being on stage, with everybody watching.*

Maybe, thought Piggy, *I'll even get a chance to do it again sometime.*